For

Suzan Pelkofsky

Thank you for the support you have given us and all the bookstore events you have arranged since our writing career began. From being business acquaintances, we have blossomed into lasting friends.

For

Arleen and Martin Richter

Thank you for believing in us and encouraging us to continue creating stories about Mrs. Belle. You are a very special couple.

-LS & SS

For

My wonderful wife, Shantel, and our fantastic children, Ciana, Jalena and Jaron.

Thank you all so much for your love and continued support. You all are the inspiration that moved me to draw each character smiling as they do.

- THB

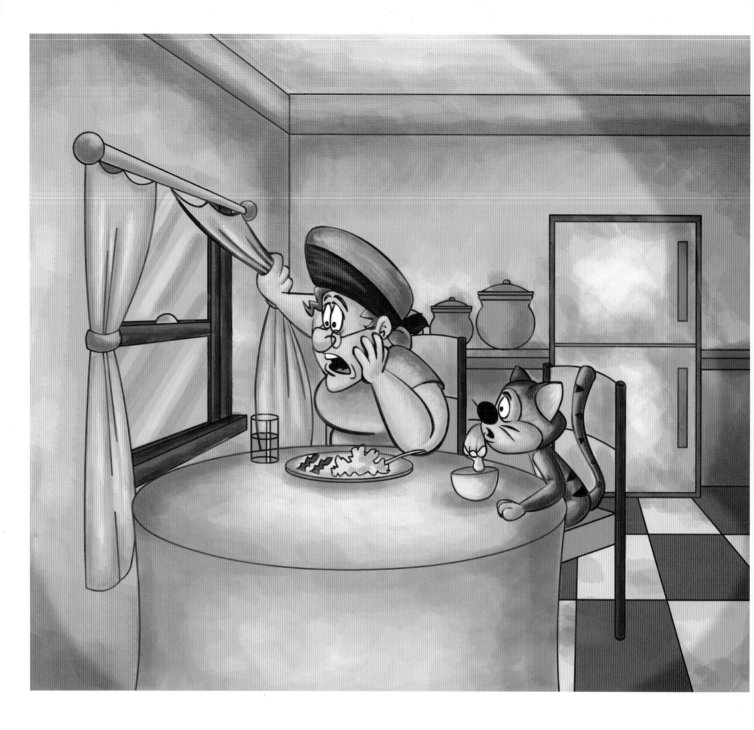

Mrs. Belle was eating breakfast when she heard loud music and noise outside her house. She looked out the window and saw the Laurelville Mayor, townspeople, and School Band marching down the street. Mrs. Belle thought, "My goodness, they're coming to my house."

She went out to the porch where Mr. Rivera and some of the children were holding signs. They all chanted:

> Mrs. Belle, when you're a MOVIE STAR,
> Fans will come to see you from near and far,
> But we will always recognize you,
> Because you'll wear your ballet shoe!

"Why are you saying that?" asked Mrs. Belle. "I'm not a movie star."

Mr. Mayor answered, "Mrs. Belle, The Marlin Movie Studio in Hollywood had a contest, and they are looking for Everybody's Favorite Teacher. The children at the Laurelville School nominated you, and GUESS WHAT?"

All the children shouted, "Mrs. Belle, you won! You won the contest! You were chosen to be Everybody's Favorite Teacher."

"Oh my, I just can't believe this is happening to me," said Mrs. Belle.

"What prize did I win?"

Mr. Rivera handed Mrs. Belle an envelope. She opened it and read the letter aloud.

Dear Mrs. Belle,

I am pleased to announce that you have been chosen to be the star of the new film, "*Everybody's Favorite Teacher*," which will be produced by the Marlin Movie Studio. I will be coming with a camera crew to Laurelville to make the biography of your life.

Congratulations and best wishes. I'm looking forward to meeting Mrs. Belle, "The Teacher Who Would Not Retire." Start getting all of your pairs of colorful ballet slippers ready. You'll be wearing them in the film. Mr. Rivera, Magic, and Kitty Belle will be in the movie too.

Sincerely,
J. T. Dommy, Film Director

The next day, Mrs. Belle went to buy some special new slippers for the filming. Mrs. Belle tried on so many pairs of ballet slippers, but she kept saying to the salesman, "No! No! No! These will not do! I'm going to be a movie star, so I must wear what an actress should wear."

Suddenly, Mr. Rivera called out, "Mrs. Belle, Mrs. Belle, I found the perfect shoes for you. Stars for a star." There, in his hands, was a pair of red, open-toed, ballet slippers with a pattern of sparkling silver stars.

"This is just perfect! Even my feet will look like I am a movie star." She told the salesperson, "Please give me six pairs in different colors."

When they left the Shoe Store, Mr. Rivera couldn't see where he was walking because the shoe boxes were piled high in his arms. Mrs. Belle was so happy, she danced down the street. She stopped short when she saw a shiny, lucky penny lying on the ground. As Mrs. Belle bent over to pick it up, Mr. Rivera bumped into her. All six boxes flew into the air, opened, and fell to the ground. What a mess! It took them ten minutes to match the pairs and box them again. Kitty Belle and Magic thought it was a game.

When Mrs. Belle returned home, there was a Trailer Truck parked in front of her house, and the townspeople were all there. The camera crew began filming as a television news reporter announced, "Here comes Mrs. Belle, "Everybody's Favorite Teacher," and with her are Mr. Rivera, and their two pets, Kitty Belle and Magic."

"Beloved Local Teacher Becomes Newest Celebrity!"

LV NEWS

The children chanted:

Mrs. Belle, when you're a MOVIE STAR,
Fans will come to see you from near and far,
But we will always recognize you,
Because you'll wear your ballet shoe!

LET THE MAKEOVER BEGIN!

No one knew what was happening in Mrs. Belle's house. Madam Anna, the greatest Makeup Artist from Hollywood, stayed in the house for three days. She closed all the doors and pulled down the window shades. What was she doing to Mrs. Belle?

Mrs. Belle's fingernails were manicured, her toenails got a pedicure, and she took a mud bath to make her skin beautiful. The Cat Groomer painted Kitty Belle's nails and put a sparkling collar on her.

Madam Anna said, "Mrs. Belle, your makeover is almost finished. Now we must find the perfect hairdo for you." She opened a large trunk and pulled out a bright, red wig that flipped all the way up on the sides.

When she set it on Mrs. Belle's head, Mrs. Belle said, "Oh no, this will not do! I look like I have wings, and I'm ready to fly away like a bird."

Then Madam Anna put a very long, black and white wig on Mrs. Belle. It flowed onto the floor. Once again, Mrs. Belle was not happy. She said, "Oh no, this will not do! I look just like a zebra in a zoo."

Madam Anna took out a third wig. This wig had short, green curls. When Mrs. Belle looked in the mirror, she cried out, "Oh no, this will not do. I look just like a head of lettuce!"

Madam Anna said, "Mrs. Belle, what are we going to do?"

Mrs. Belle answered, "I won the contest to be "Everybody's Favorite Teacher" because the children love me the way I am. Please let me wear my own hair. It would be just perfect!"

Madam Anna said, "Mrs. Belle, you are a very smart woman. Yes, the children do love you the way you are."

The school gym was set up as a movie studio, and on the first day of the filming, J.T. Dommy invited all the children to come watch Mrs. Belle act.

The room was dark, and suddenly they heard the Director shout,

"LIGHTS! CAMERA! ACTION!"

There in the spotlight was Mr. Rivera, narrating the film. "This is the biography of a very special person. You will see some of the highlights of Mrs. Belle's life. When Mrs. Belle was only one year old, she knew how to count her little fingers and BIG toes. Her mother just knew she was going to be a teacher when she grew up."

Then the spotlight was on a baby carriage, and there, in it, was a baby, with two stuffed animals: a cat and a dog.

"Look," shouted the children, "Kitty Belle and Magic are movie stars, too." Then they looked closer at the baby. IT WAS A BIG BABY! And it was real! It was Mrs. Belle! The only shoes that would fit her when she was a baby were ballet slippers with openings in the front for her big toes to stick out.

Mr. Rivera continued, "Now we see how Mrs. Belle got her love for Ballet Slippers."

All the children laughed and said:

Mrs. Belle, when you're a MOVIE STAR,
Fans will come to see you from near and far,
But we will always recognize you,
Because you'll wear your ballet shoe!

For a whole week, Mrs. Belle, Mr. Rivera, Kitty Belle, and Magic reported to the studio in the Gym. They rehearsed many scenes about Mrs. Belle's life as a teacher. Her favorite one was when she and Mr. Rivera stayed up all night and baked 100 cakes for the PTA to sell at the Laurelville School Cake Sale. The money they raised helped to buy new books for the school library. Poor Kitty Belle and Magic were covered from head to toe with white flour.

There were even scenes showing Mrs. Belle having fun snorkeling with the children at the Laurelville Camp and also going with her space team to the new Pink Planet she discovered.

Finally, the movie was completed. Mrs. Belle was so tired, but she was also very happy.

Everyone in town received a special invitation that said:

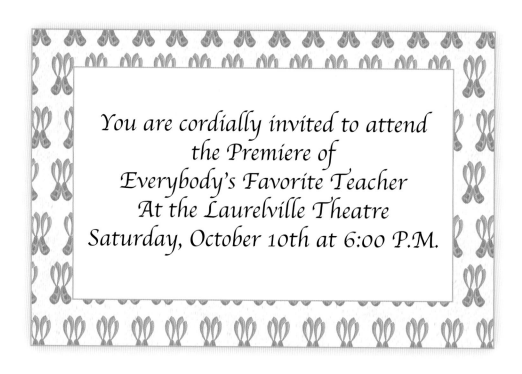

You are cordially invited to attend
the Premiere of
Everybody's Favorite Teacher
At the Laurelville Theatre
Saturday, October 10th at 6:00 P.M.

On the day of the Premiere, Mr. Rivera and Magic arrived at Mrs. Belle's house in a black Limousine. How handsome they both looked in their tuxedos.

Mrs. Belle and Kitty Belle came down the path wearing identical outfits. Mrs. Belle said, "Oh Mr. Rivera, I feel like a Fairy Princess." Her beautiful pink gown had sparkling, silver stars to match her open-toed, ballet slippers, and on her head was a diamond crown.

Mr. Rivera asked Mrs. Belle to wear a blindfold until they got to the theatre.

When the limousine arrived at the Premiere, Mrs. Belle heard all the children chanting:

Mrs. Belle, when you're a MOVIE STAR,
Fans will come to see you from near and far,
But we will always recognize you,
Because you'll wear your ballet shoe!

Mrs. Belle removed the blindfold, looked up at the Marquee, and smiled. The Laurelville Theatre was now the Mrs. Belle Theatre. She said, "I can't believe I have a theatre named after me."

As they walked down the red carpet, the children giggled. Mrs. Belle saw all her friends, both old and new.

Mr. Mayor called out, "Mrs. Belle, please come here."

Everyone clapped because there in the center of the lobby, was a huge, gold statue of Mrs. Belle.

Below the statue it said:

THIS THEATRE IS DEDICATED TO A VERY SPECIAL PERSON
MRS. BELLE
EVERYBODY'S FAVORITE TEACHER

And they all went in to see the movie!

THE NURSE DISGUISE

THE CONSTRUCTION WORKER DISGUISE

MRS. BELLES CAT

THE TRAPEZE ARTIST DISGUISE

NO DISGUISE! THE ORIGINAL MRS. BELLE

THE JAZZ PLAYER DISGUISE